NO TIME *for* ME

By
JOHN M. BARRETT

Illustrated by
JOE SERVELLO

HUMAN SCIENCES PRESS
72 Fifth Avenue   3 Henrietta Street
NEW YORK, NY 10011 ● LONDON, WC2E 8LU

For Mary Craig

Library of Congress Cataloguing in Publication Data

Barrett, John M   No time for me.
     SUMMARY: With both parents working, life
changes for Jimmy and he feels neglected and
hostile.   1.   Children of working parents—United States—
Juvenile literature.   2.   Parent and child—
Juvenile literature.   [1.   Mothers—Employment.
2.   Parent and child.   3.   Family life]
I.   Servello, Joe.   II.   Title.
HQ 755.85.B37   301.42'7   78-21257
ISBN   0-87705-385-5

My name is James, but that's my Dad's name too, so everybody calls me Jimmy. I'm eight years old and in the third grade. This year on the first day of school, when we had to write down our parents' jobs and phone numbers, it was easy for me. I could put down 'Lawyer' under 'Father' and 'Lawyer' under 'Mother'. I laughed when our teacher said that the kids who couldn't spell 'Housewife' could write 'Mom' for their mothers. I laughed and felt proud that now my mother had a real job.

A few weeks later I stopped laughing. I stopped laughing but I
didn't know why. School was okay, and my friends still liked me,
but every day I felt a little bit sadder. Then I got mad at myself for
being sad, but that didn't do any good. Mom and Dad were so busy
that they never really noticed, and I didn't tell them.

I couldn't figure out what was going wrong with me until it was
time for Parents' Visiting Day at school. Dad could never come
because he worked in the city, but Mom always came. I liked her
to see my desk, my papers on the bulletin board, and my teacher.
School is my job and office.

This year, after dinner, when I gave Mom the note about the visiting day, she looked worried. As she checked her appointment book, she shook her head and said sadly, "I'm sorry, Jimmy, but I have to be in court that morning. My client needs me too. I can't miss his trial. I've gone to school all the other years, but I have a job now. Can you understand that?"

I nodded, swallowed back my tears, and went upstairs to finish my arithmetic. I saw my sister Kim come out of my room. I yelled at her, "You stay out of there. You baby shrimp!" She ran away from me.

As I sat down at my desk, my tears came out. "It's not fair. It's not fair," I cried to myself. "Dad's gone all the time. Now Mom is gone too. There's just no time for me in this family. No time for me!" I shoved my arithmetic book off the desk and fell onto my bed. I lay on my stomach, with my arms around my pillow, and I fell asleep.

Dad woke me in the morning with his gentle touch and his usual, "Good morning, Champ. Time to get up." He sat on my bed and added, "Mom and I let you sleep in your clothes last night because you were so tired. You'd better put on some clean ones for today, though. Those really do look like you slept in them!"

I started to tell Dad that I was sad, not tired, that I missed him, and now I missed Mom too. I was going to tell him that I loved him, and ask him to come to Parents' Visiting Day—but I didn't get a chance. Before I could say anything, he gave me a pat on the back and said, "Sorry Champ. I've got to run, or I'll miss my train. If I don't see you tonight, I'll see you tomorrow morning."

"See you, Dad," I slowly answered, getting out of bed. After breakfast Mom asked, "Jimmy, are you feeling better?" I answered, "Sure," kissed her good-by, and took Kim to school.

Parents' Visiting Day came, but nobody came for me. I felt like an orphan without Mom or Dad. Then I saw that Tommy's parents weren't there either. At recess and on the way home from school Tommy and I talked. He told me that he felt sad a lot of the time too, especially last year, when his parents got divorced and his father moved to another town. He said that you always feel sad when you lose something.

Tommy was right, and talking with him that day made me feel better. We became best friends. Almost every day we played after school, and some Fridays we slept overnight at his house or my house. Before falling asleep we would pillow fight and wrestle. Then we'd be tired and quiet, and we'd talk about what we liked and what we hated. When I was with Tommy I didn't miss my parents so much.

Tommy told me that he saw his parents the most on weekends. Sometimes his Mom or Dad took him to a game, a museum, or even camping. That gave me an idea! Dad and Mom had asked me what I wanted for my birthday. Now I knew. I wanted to go to a Yale football game. We had gone once before and had the best time— a picnic, pennants, popcorn, and everything.

When I told Mom and Dad what I wanted for my birthday, they were as happy as I was. Dad checked the schedule and found that the last game in November was on my birthday. He asked if I wanted to bring a friend, and of course I said, "Tommy!"

When the tickets came, Dad let me keep them in my desk. I looked at them every night, and crossed off that day on my calendar. Soon it would be my birthday, and I'd be with my family and Tommy at a football game—all at the same time.

One Sunday evening, about three weeks before my birthday, I noticed Mom and Dad looking nervously at each other. Finally Dad began to talk. "Jimmy, I know how much you're looking forward to the game—for your birthday—and with Tommy—and everyone. Your mother and I have been too."

I quickly answered. "Sure Dad. I can hardly wait. There's only one—."

"Well, son," he interrupted, "there's been a slight change of plans. You'll still be going, and so will Tommy and Kim, but with Grandma and Grandpa—not with us."

I felt the hot tears coming to my eyes, and I cried, "Why? Why? What's so important? A dinner party? The opera? Your offices? What?"

He put his hand on my shoulder and said, "Listen Jimmy, I'm sorry too. Please understand. There's a lawyers' meeting that I can't miss. I'm giving a talk. Mr. Skidmore was supposed to go, but he's in the hospital."

Fighting back the tears, I asked, "What about Mom? Why can't she go to the game? She likes football as much as you."

Dad bit his lip and said, "Jimmy, this meeting is down in the Virgin Islands, and your mother is going with me. She needs a change, and there are important meetings for her too. Your grandparents will stay here that week, and they'll take you to the game."

Mom reached for my hand, which was now a tight fist. "I'm sorry your birthday, the game, and our trip are all at the same time, Jimmy, but we can have a big party when we come back, and next year we'll all go to a game together."

"Sure we will," I said, hardly able to talk. I pulled my hand away from my mother. Mumbling, "Excuse me," I went up to my room.

As I slowly walked upstairs, I heard my mother say to my father, "Do you think I should go up and talk to him? He's so upset."

My father answered, "I wouldn't. He's got to learn to live with disappointment some day."

"Those liars," I said to myself, "they don't do anything for me." I slammed my door and undressed with the lights off.

Neither Mom nor Dad came to my room right away, but Kim did. She opened the door without knocking and came over to my bed. She said, "What's wrong, Jimmy? Don't you like me? Don't you like Grandma and Grandpa?"

I pulled her close to me and hugged her, saying, "Sure I do. But Mom and Dad promised to take me to the game for my birthday, and I wanted to go with them, so we'd be together. That's all."

Kim softly said, "Oh," and kissed me on the cheek. As she went out, she turned and whispered, "Good night, Jimmy." When my mother and later my father looked in on me and quietly called my name, I pretended to be asleep.

In the morning when Dad woke me up, he stayed in my room longer than usual. He rubbed my back and started to tickle me like he did when I was little. It was fun until he said, "You know, Jimmy, you don't always get exactly what you want in life. Things change, and you have to change too. Your mother and I understand how disappointed you are, and we'll make it up to you. Okay?"

I didn't feel like talking, so I just said, "Okay, Dad," and got out of bed. As I was looking around for some clothes to wear, he put his arm around my shoulder and said, "Thanks, Jim."

I didn't know what he was thanking me for. I said again, "It's *okay,* Dad," and he left the room.

I didn't bother to look at the football tickets that night or any other night. I didn't cross off the days on the calendar anymore either. Even so, the days went quickly, and soon my grandparents came. We all went to the airport to wave good-by to Mom and Dad. It felt good to see everyone else crying a little, and not be the only one.

Kim and I loved having Grandma and Grandpa stay with us. They were like parents, but even better because they were always there. Grandpa made our favorite chocolate cake with thick frosting, and Grandma told us the stories of her life on the farm when she was a girl.

When Tommy met Grandma and Grandpa, he asked them, "Do you know why elephants are grey?" They didn't know. When he said, "So you can tell that they aren't blueberries!" they laughed and laughed.

I had my best birthday, ever, that Saturday at the football game. Yale won 18–12. Tommy and I yelled and cheered the whole time. When we stopped for dinner afterwards, there was a cake for me at the restaurant, and everyone sang. I easily blew the candles out and kept my wish a secret, even from Tommy. As we kids were falling asleep in the back seat on the way home, I wondered why I had been so upset when Mom and Dad couldn't go to the game.

On Sunday I thought I was going to be happy for the rest of my life. Everything had gone so well, and Mom and Dad were coming home that afternoon. Grandma, Grandpa, Kim, and I were playing Monopoly, when I heard a car pull into the driveway. Before we knew it, Mom and Dad were there in the family room, suntanned and smiling. They looked younger than I remembered them, a lot younger than Grandma and Grandpa.

Dad reached down and picked up Kim, and I hugged Mom and
gave her a kiss. For some reason I started crying, like I did at the
airport.

Kim yelled, "Mommy!" and Dad handed her to Mom.

Dad knelt down to me, and I put my arms around him and kissed him. I was still crying, and before I knew what I was doing, I started hitting him with my fists and kicking him, as hard as I could. He had his arms around me and just held me tighter.

I screamed at him, "You left me here! You didn't care about my birthday! You don't care about me! All you care about are yourselves and your jobs. There's no time for me in this family! I hate you! I hate you! I hate you! I'm not your son anymore. I'm leaving."

I tried to hit him and kick him some more, but he picked me up and held me close to him so that I couldn't. He didn't say anything but "Jimmy, Jimmy," as he rocked me back and forth.

I cried and cried and cried. I didn't feel like hurting Dad anymore. Then I didn't feel like crying anymore either. I heard Grandma say, "I don't know what happened to him. He's been so perfect all week." I heard Grandma, Grandpa, and Kim leave the room. I said to Dad, "Let me go, Dad. I'm all right now." Dad let me go, and I could see he'd been crying too. So had Mom.

Dad wiped his eyes with his hand and said, "Jimmy, these last few months we haven't been working very well as a family. One thing we all must do is talk more about what we're feeling inside. I had no idea you were so angry and hurt by our missing your birthday. And that's only part of the problem."

"Dad," I quickly interrupted, "you would have gone on that trip anyway. I know you and Mom."

"That's right," Mom responded, "we had to go—and we went. But if we had really talked before we went, and even planned some other trips—for all of us—you might not have felt so bad."

I half-smiled and sighed, saying, "Maybe you're right."

"It's true," Mom continued, "that things haven't been the same since I started working. We've all been very busy. It's hard to do everything we used to do."

Dad smiled and said, "A big family calendar for the kitchen might help us plan a little better. We'll write down everybody's important dates, way in advance. And the first thing I'll be writing down is a five-day ski trip for all of us in December. I'll—."

"Dad," I broke in, "do you think you could come home from work early some nights, so we could all have spaghetti dinners in the kitchen together?"

Dad looked right into my eyes without a word. Then he said, "I can come home early most Wednesday nights, Jimmy, and some mornings I can wake you up half-an-hour before I leave, so we can have breakfast together. I want to be with you more too."

"Yes," Mom said. "We can't quit our jobs, but we can talk more and plan more things to do together."

"Can we read stories at night like we used to?" I asked. "Scarey ones?"

"As long as I can keep the lights on," Mom answered, laughing.

"Thanks, Mom," I said with a smile. "Thanks, Dad."

I jumped into their arms. We hugged and kissed each other. I was glad they were home.

"Let's go find everyone else," I suggested. "Grandpa made a Birthday—Welcome Home cake, and I'm ready for a giant piece."

We walked into the kitchen and joined the rest of the family around the table. While we ate our cake and ice cream, everyone talked or asked questions about the Virgin Islands or the football game. Kim asked, "Why are elephants grey?" We laughed a lot, and I felt like it was my birthday all over again.